DIARY

Basketball
Hero

Shamini Flint

Illustrated by Sally Heinrich

ALLEN&UNWIN

SYDNEY • MELBOURNE • AUCKLAND • LONDON

This edition published in 2015

First published in Singapore in 2014 by Sunbear Publishing

Allen & Unwin
83 Alexander Street
Crows Nest NSW 2065
Australia
Phone: (61 2) 8425 0100
Email: info@allenandunwin.com
Web: www.allenandunwin.com

A Cataloguing-in-Publication entry is available
from the National Library of Australia
www.trove.nla.gov.au

ISBN 978 1 76011 150 2

Text design by Sally Heinrich
Series cover concept by Jaime Harrison
Set in 12/14 pt Comic Sans

This book was printed in March 2019 at McPherson's Printing Group, 76 Nelson St, Maryborough, Victoria 3465, Australia.
www.mcphersonsprinting.com.au

15 14 13 12

MY BASKETBALL DIARY

I actually know how to play basketball.

You just need to throw a ball into a basket.

No problem.

Watch this!

See how well I'm doing?
SEE????

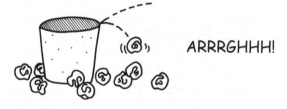

ARRRGHHH!

Why would Dad think that I could play
basketball?

I have trouble getting rubbish into the
rubbish bin.

Dad thinks I might be able to play basketball because I accidentally bounced a golf ball into a hole.

That's like thinking I can paint like Van Gogh because I once drew a stick figure of a man with one ear.

Or that I'm ready to pilot a space shuttle to Mars because I once made a paper aeroplane.

Or that because I climbed a tree in the garden, I'm ready to plant my flag on top of Mt Everest.

It's just ridiculous …

You see, Dad believes that I have a gift for sport.

> Marcus is very good at sport!

It doesn't matter that I have failed at so many, many, MANY sports.
He just thinks that I haven't tried the right sport yet!

> We just haven't found the right sport, Son!

Seriously, Dad?

Surely we can agree on just a few things by now?

How about we agree that, I, Marcus Atkinson, aged nine …

Am rubbish at sports involving balls?

Am hopeless at games involving bats?

Am bad on land … and in water?

Talking to Dad is like talking to a brick wall ...

or a robot.

Talking to Dad is like talking to animals!

Woof!!!

whine....

Sorry, Spot – I didn't mean you.
I know you understand that I'm rubbish at sport.

I think basketball is going to be your game!

I'm sure of it!

Sigh...

Marcus, what are you doing?
You haven't made a fool of yourself yet!
Why are you in here with a paper bag over your head?
I thought I might as well get started early . . .
as this is the way it usually ends.

The problem is that Dad has written a book. It's called *Pull Yourself Up by Your Own Bootstraps*.

It's full of useful advice. NOT.

Even I could write a book with better advice in it!!!

My advice:

Stay away from sharks. They're dangerous.

Dad's advice:

A shark is just a fish— you have nothing to fear but fear itself.

My advice:

Dad's advice:

My advice:

Dad's advice:

Good plan, Dad. And what about food and shelter and water and school and friends and LIFE?????

So I give good advice and Dad gives rubbish advice but people queue up around the block to buy his book.

All I write are these diaries that no one will ever read.

Gemma, my older sister, reads my diaries and leaves me comments on Post-it notes.

I used to try to hide the diaries but it's no use ...

Even if I dug a hole to the centre of the planet and hid my new diary there, she'd find it.

Even if I swum to the bottom of the ocean and hid it, she'd find it.

Even if I took a rocket to the end of the universe and hid it there, she'd find it.

You're quite right!

The good news is that Dad couldn't find me a golf coach last time round.

The bad news is that Dad decided to coach me himself.

13

The only sure way to avoid any further failure is if Dad can't find a coach.

I need some luck.

The only way to get some luck is to get some lucky stuff!

I'm onto it!!

Let's see:

I have a lucky number 7 ...

A four-leaf clover ...

A horseshoe ...

Lucky for you, not so lucky for the horse?

I'll throw some salt over my shoulder ...

Okay, maybe they didn't mean the salt shaker too.
Oops.

I just need a rainbow
and then there's no
way Dad will find a
coach ...

Good point!!

Thanks, Gemma.

BASKETBALL LESSON NO. 1

It turns out that none of the coaches of boys' teams would have me.

Coach Jane is a friend of Dad's.

She agreed to take me.

I'm playing basketball with girls.

There's only one way to survive this ...

no one must know.

I must keep this a
secret until I die.

And it must remain a
secret after I die.

School the next day seemed all right. No one was laughing at me.

My secret was still safe ... PHEW!!

BASKETBALL LESSON NO. 2

What sort of names are those??

It turns out they've named themselves after famous basketball players. I call that lame, so there.

We will start with slaps.

Slap? These girls? Does Coach think I'm stupid?

Maybe a gentle pat to the back?

Ball slaps!

What did the ball ever do to me??

This is easy!

I can do this!

Maybe basketball is my sport!

Finger pads?
Fingers on iPads?

I'd like to build a brick wall around me.

BASKETBALL LESSON NO. 3

34

The next day was my big SuperChef for Kids moment (read my *Diary of a Golf Pro* if you're not sure how I came to be taking part in a cooking contest).

I'd practised everything with Mum from breads to burgers, cupcakes to casseroles, salads to stews. I could bake, boil, fry, grill and steam.

Unfortunately ...

the task was to boil an egg!!!!

To be more precise, a soft-boiled egg.

I did my best.
But my best wasn't good enough.

My goose was cooked ...

Could things get any worse???

Stupid question.

Of course they can ...

BASKETBALL LESSON NO. 4

Note to Dad –
things I enjoy:

Playing video games ...

Skipping school ...

Lying in a hammock ...

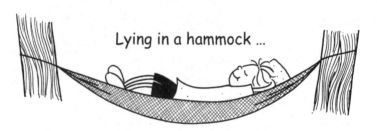

Things I do not enjoy:

Playing basketball ...

Playing a basketball match ...

Playing basketball in a girls' team ...

Playing a basketball match in a girls'
team against kids from my school ...

Playing a basketball match ... against Hulk!!

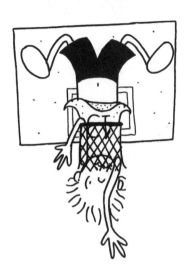

BASKETBALL GAME NO. 1

How bad was it? Well, no one died.
Aside from that, it was pretty bad.

It started quite well.

No one passed me the ball.

I got out of the
way as much as
I could.

The girls were amazing.

Girls are
always
amazing.
Gemma

Kobe hit a three (you get three points in basketball for shots taken from outside the D)!

Magic blocked a shot that was definitely going in!

Jordan passed the ball round her back to LeBron!

Did I mention that I stayed out of the way as much as I could?

And then Kobe clashed with Hulk. The ball popped out of her hands. It rolled towards me.

I picked it up. And stood there for a while.

There's a shot clock?

I looked around for a pass but no one was free.

Phew! I remember when I thought 'dribble' was that thing baby Harriet did.

But I knew what to do this time!

We turned over possession.

The boys were winning!

I had to do something.

Sadly, I got the ball.

Marcus, do something!

I looked up. The basket was so far I could barely see it. There was no way I could score from here.

I ran forward.
I had to get closer!

Travelling?

Where does he think I'm going?

Mind you, I'd love to travel away from this game ...

How about to Alaska? Or the Gobi Desert? Or the Great Barrier Reef?

Apparently, you're not allowed to take any steps in basketball without bouncing the ball.

Who knew that?

We turned over possession. They scored.

I went back to doing nothing.

LeBron tried a three-pointer that came off the rim.

The ball landed at my feet. I pretended not to notice.

50

That was as clear as mud.

Kobe came to visit the next day.

Had she just come to rub it in?

We sat in silence for a while. I still had no idea why Kobe had come around.

Kobe left. I waved goodbye.
I still had no idea why she had come to visit.

Dad came home then. Phew!

BASKETBALL LESSON NO. 5

Has she been reading Dad's book?

If at first you don't succeed, keep doing the same thing because it gives people something to laugh at ...

I missed the basket again ...

It really is pretty cool – if you're taller than a giraffe!!!

Does Coach think there'll be tastefully scattered ladders on the court in our next game?

I do not.

Kobe taught me a few neat tricks ...

Oh! I knew that. NOT.

Next, we tried shooting ...

But actually, I'm a bit worried about this Kobe thing.

Why did she visit?
Why is she giving me basketball lessons?

Why is she laughing at my jokes?

No one does that!!

What if she wants to get married???

I'm too young!!!!!

Most weeks, I just need to run away from home because of sports.

Now I need to run away because of girls as well?

I'll need to go somewhere without girls ...

The army?

Prison?

The South Pole?

BASKETBALL GAME NO. 2

I had that feeling of déjà vu all over again.

Parents – check.

Sisters – check.

Friends – check.

Banners – check.

Coach – check.

Team – check.

Girlfriend – check.

Hi, Marcus!

AARRRRGGGGHH!!!

FIRST QUARTER

LeBron scored a three-point jump shot.

Magic dribbled the ball from hand to hand, through her legs, back again and passed for another two points.

Kobe scored a lay-up.

DOUBLE WOW!!

TRIPLE WOW!!!

But the boys matched us point for point.

Kobe kept trying to pass to me but I looked the other way.

I only touched the ball once ...

The referee awarded them two free throws. He seemed to think I fell over the ball on purpose.

I guess even he can't believe how rubbish I am.

Hulk made both free throws.

At the end of first quarter – the boys were winning by two points.

SECOND QUARTER

The first thing Kobe did was win the jump ball.

The second thing she did was pass me the ball. PANIC!!!

I threw it right back at her.

She scored a fadeaway jumper.

I just threw the ball right back at her.
She must really like me.
Or she wouldn't think that was a great pass.

I DON'T WANT TO
GET MARRIED!!!

They scored, we* scored, they scored, we* scored.
*When I say 'we', I do not mean 'me'.

One of the boys made a fast break.

I remembered everything I had learnt ... from rugby.

Three free throws.

Apparently, rugby is not a useful guide to basketball.

HALF-TIME

We were now five points behind.

I didn't need anyone to tell me that I'd given away all the fouls for those five points.

THIRD QUARTER

I think that was code for 'don't let Marcus touch the ball'.

Magic cut to the left, faked a couple of defenders with a crossover dribble and scored!

LeBron dribbled into the paint and was fouled by Hulk.

She scored both free throws.

Kobe tried a hook shot, the ball came off the rim, hit me on the head and bounced to Hulk. He scored at the other end.

The boys were matching us point for point. And they were still five points ahead.

Only one quarter to go.

The girls discussed tactics.
Coach discussed tactics.
I sat quietly at the other end of the bench.

Kobe slid over.

I slid a bit further over.
She followed me.

I was getting desperate. There was only one thing to do.

Try Gemma's plan.

Just tell her about your bad habits - that should drive her away!

I never wash behind my ears!

What?

And I pick my nose a lot!!

What??

And I rarely change my underpants!!!

Ewww!!!

You really do remind me of my brother, Jonathan.

Eh?

Hey, Jon, come over and say 'hi'.

NOT!!

I decided I didn't like Kobe's brother after all.

Another chap turned up.

PHEW!!!
I don't have to have a
girlfriend!!!

I DON'T HAVE TO GET MARRIED!!!

FOURTH QUARTER

Five minutes to play.
Five points to make up.

Everyone looked surprised.

Kobe reacted quickest.

She passed me the ball.

I remembered what she'd said. Throw in an arc. Use the angle of the backboard.

I went for it!
Three points!!

Hulk went on a run. He changed directions so many times, I felt dizzy.

LeBron managed to block his shot.

The ball fell at my feet.
I picked it up.

I looked up. She
was way down by
the basket.

I flung the ball
with all my might.

Kobe grabbed it
and scored!

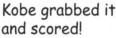

One point
between the
teams!!

Sixty seconds left!!!

Hulk faked a shot.

I fell for it and knocked
the ball out of his hand.

Thirty seconds on the clock.

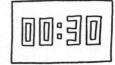

Hulk made the first throw.

He made the second.

Three points between the teams!!

TIME-OUT

Coach called a time-out.

We huddled. We needed three points to tie the game and go into overtime.

Fifteen seconds left.

LeBron faked a defence and passed to Kobe.

Kobe made a bounce pass to Magic.

I sprinted down
the paint.

Kobe pivoted and looped the ball to me. I stared at the basket – it seemed so far away.

The girls screened me.

I lined up the shot ...

OVERTIME

We were back on the court.

Magic won the jump off.
No surprise.

The girls passed to each other.

The girls passed to each other some more.

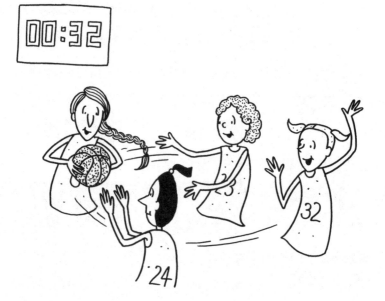

Take the shot!!!

00:20

Kobe tried a three-pointer.
It came off the rim.

Luckily, Magic won the rebound.
There are definitely advantages
to being taller than everyone.

Marcus, now!!

32

I sprinted forward.

Kobe dribbled away from the basket where we needed to score.

Kobe turned and lobbed the ball towards me.

There was no way I was going to catch it.
It was too high!

But that's where Kobe's plan came in.
I leapt forward.

Magic gave me a
huge heave!!

I soared through the air ...

and caught the ball.

I turned three somersaults (that wasn't in the plan) ...

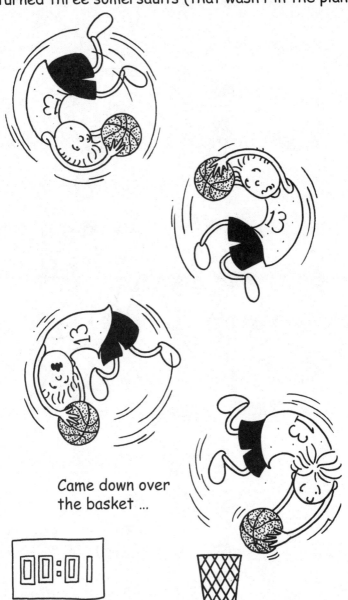

Came down over
the basket ...

00:01

About the Author

Shamini Flint lives in Singapore with her husband and two children. She is an ex-lawyer, ex-lecturer, stay-at-home mum and writer. She loves basketball!

www.shaminiflint.com

Have you read all of my other diaries?